KU-324-416

THIS WALKER BOOK BELONGS TO:

_____

_____

_____

_____

STAFFORDSHIRE LIBRARIES

3 8014 03867 1589

STAFFORDSHIRE LIBRARIES ARTS AND ARCHIVES	
38014038671589	
PET	02-Dec-04
823.91	£4.99
BURT	

For Rosie – of course, and Polly too.
J.H.

For Audrey Keri-Nagy and her little Rose.
H.C.

First published 2002 by Walker Books Ltd
87 Vauxhall Walk, London SE11 5HJ

This edition published 2003

2 4 6 8 10 9 7 5 3 1

Text © 2002 Judy Hindley
Illustrations © 2002 Helen Craig Ltd

The right of Judy Hindley and Helen Craig to be identified as
author and illustrator respectively of this work has been asserted by
them in accordance with the Copyright, Designs and Patents Act 1988

This book has been typeset in Poliphilus MT

Printed in China

All rights reserved

British Library Cataloguing in Publication Data:
a catalogue record for this book is available from the British Library

ISBN 0-7445-9809-5

ROSY'S VISITORS

JUDY HINDLEY

illustrated by HELEN CRAIG

WALKER BOOKS
AND SUBSIDIARIES
LONDON • BOSTON • SYDNEY

One day Rosy said,
"Today is moving day.
I'm going to find myself
a whole new house."
She packed up her blanket
and her pillow, and her
books and toys, and
all her favourite things …
and started looking.

Then
they came
in the house and
tried out everything.
They all loved Rosy's house.
They had a tremendous feast,
and they sang and they danced …

till they were so tired out they had to leave.

"Goodbye! Goodbye!" they called.

"Come again!" cried Rosy.

When they had gone,
Rosy had lots of
tidying to do.
Then she packed up
her things, looked
through her spyglass
one last time …

and went back home,
and she was just in time for supper.

"Welcome to my house!" cried Rosy.
Rosy's visitors came up the path
and rang the bell, and said hello.
They bowed and curtsied, and they
all brought gifts because
it was their first visit.

And there they were.
There were Rosy's visitors, coming in
from the sea, and down from the sky,
and all across the land ...
to Rosy's house.

Rosy took her spyglass
and looked out of the window.
With her spyglass
she could see far, far away.
She could see far across the
land and out over the sea,
and way up high,
high into the sky.

Then she said, "Now I
need a bell for visitors to ring."
She found a jingle-bell and
hung it by the door.
"There!" she said. "Now
everything is perfect. I'm
ready for visitors. I wonder
if anyone will come."

"Hmm," said Rosy. "I wonder if visitors will find my house. I think I just need a path, so visitors can find the way." She found some stones and things, and marked a path right up to her front door.

When she was finished,
Rosy clapped her hands.
"This is my house,
it's Rosy's house!"
she sang.
And she put up a sign
so everyone could
see that this was
Rosy's house.

She hung up her coat and
rain hat and she made her bed.
She found a special place to
sit and think, or draw,
or read her book.

Rosy got busy.
"This is my house; it's mine,
all mine!" she sang.
She swept and
tidied her
house, and
made it neat.

Very soon she found a little house.
She peeked in through the door.
She looked all around.
"This is it! This is my house!"
cried Rosy. "What a
perfect house."